Minton Goes!

DRIVING

Anna Fienberg and Kim Gamble

ALLEN&UNWIN

Minton was thinking about wheels.

'Vroom vroom,' he said under his breath. He wanted to make a car *now*.

But he was sitting at a café in the city. It was his friend Bouncer's favourite place.

'A beetle and banana milkshake, please,' he told the waiter.

'We're fresh out of beetles,' the waiter said sadly. 'How about our special — mango and millipede malt?'

Minton nodded. 'Vroom vroom,' he said to the sugar bowl. '*EEEeek!*'

'Sssh!' Turtle scowled. 'Do you want to get us thrown out of here?'

'I was doing the screeching tyres bit,' explained Minton.

Minton looked around the café. His car would be yellow – a jaunty jeep maybe? When he'd lived by the sea with Turtle, it had been easy to find what he needed to build things. But where would you start in the city?

As the door to the kitchen swung open, he spied some empty jars in the bin. They had terrific lids.

'Excuse me,' he said to his friends, and tiptoed into the kitchen. 'Is anyone using these fantastic lids?' he asked the cook.

'Nope,' said the cook. 'Go for your life.'

'Is anyone using these old meat skewers?'

'Nope,' said the cook. 'Go for your life.'

'Is anyone using these old butter tubs?'

'Nope,' said the cook. 'But don't eat 'em all at once.'

When Minton got back
to the table, he spread his
treasure out.

'Bingo!' he cried, rolling four
lids across the table. 'Here are
my wheels!'

'Uh oh,' sighed Turtle,
catching one.

'And here are my axles, see?'
Minton held up a skewer.

'What if your car zooms out
of control,' said Turtle, 'and goes
crashing into a skyscraper and
blows up?'

The waiter brought a candle to the table. Outside, the city lights sparkled in a navy sky.

'Ah,' cried Bouncer. 'Good food and good friends. This is the life!'

But Minton was looking at the dead match lying on the napkin. No one would need that. And he might just be able to use it for a handbrake.

Minton hauled his toolbox up onto the table. He took out some scissors and sticky tape.

'Couldn't you at least wait until we've had our earthworm pudding with firefly sauce?' sighed Turtle.

That night, back at the caravan, Turtle yawned and
slipped into bed.

But Minton wanted to work. He began cutting
out the doors for his jeep.

'Will you put out the light now?' said Turtle. 'Some of us around here want to sleep.'

So Minton worked by torchlight. It was a bit hard getting the wheels on while holding a torch.

At midnight, the car was almost finished.

Minton just had to wake Turtle up to show him.

'*I* would have painted it white,' Turtle said. 'White cars are easier to see at night. As it is, enormous trucks and buses will crash into you for sure.'

Minton went to look for a bumper bar.

At sunrise Minton was ready to go for a test drive. But Turtle was too sleepy. 'Go on, tootle off in your speed machine,' he said, closing his eyes again. 'Look out for walls.'

So Minton skipped off to Bouncer's tent.

'It's a dream machine!' cried Bouncer. 'An ace roadster. A supercharger!'

'Well, I wouldn't go that far,' said Minton. But he looked pleased.

Bouncer did a double somersault and landed in the passenger seat. 'Come on, let's go!'

They headed out into the traffic.

Minton roared, 'vroom vroom!' as they sped down the street. Bouncer taught Minton all the road rules, like stopping at a red light and waving politely at the policeman.

The car whizzed along perfectly. It handled the curves, smooth as butter. It hugged the corners like a glove. No enormous trucks or buses crashed into them.

'You're a first class driver, Minton,' said Bouncer.

At morning tea time they stopped at a pirate playground. Bouncer dashed to the swings. Minton ate his sandwiches behind the wheel. 'A car is definitely the best way to get around,' he said dreamily, tooting the horn.

Bouncer and Minton were almost back at the caravan when they came to a huge hill. They car puffed and pooped its way up.

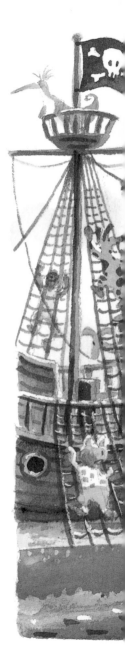

'This is more of a mountain than a hill,' said Minton.

'Don't worry, we'll make it,' said Bouncer.

At the top Milton smiled. 'A dream machine,' he said fondly.

Then he gasped. They were flying downhill.

But it wasn't the speed that worried Minton. It was the wobble.

'My wheel's coming off!' he screamed.

The car swung out all over the road. The wheel bounced free.

Minton groaned. Now he could see the caravan park. All around it were cars, vans, enormous trucks. He couldn't stop. He couldn't steer.

'Help!' he shrieked.

He looked around wildly. He was going to crash into a postal van. Then he saw something at the bottom. A round hard bump. He was heading straight for it.

'A speed hump!' he cried. '*Bouncerrr!*'

They hit the bump and sailed gracefully over the top, coming to a stop just a bumper bar away from the van.

'I always wanted to be a speed hump,' sniffed Turtle.

'Or a ski jump,' suggested Bouncer.

Minton put an arm around his neck.

'Thanks, Turtle. Are you all right?'

'I'll live,' said Turtle. 'I suppose,'

After lunch Minton fixed the wheel back on. 'There! Nothing could pull this wheel off. Not even a monster wind. *Now* will you come with me?' he asked Turtle.

They drove to the shops and looked at car radios. At the end of the street was a building site. Minton stopped. He watched an excavator as big as a dinosaur scoop up rocks in its toothy bucket.

'Will you look at that machine!' he gasped.

A loud *beep, beep, beep* filled the air as a gigantic truck backed up towards the excavator.

'Beep, beep, beep,' said Minton to himself softly. He hurried over to the man. 'Excuse me,' he said, 'but I would like to work on this building site. In fact, I can't wait.'

'You'll need a truck then,' said the man scratching his chin.

'I know,' agreed Minton. 'That's not a problem.'

'Uh oh,' said Turtle. 'No shut-eye again tonight.'

But Minton was already searching for truck parts. What could he use to make the dumper?

How to make Minton's car

To make Minton's car you'll need: 2 margarine or butter tubs and a li[...]
2 bamboo skewers, 2 corks, 4 plastic lids, glu[...]
tape, paint, and scissors or a sharp kni[...]

1. Make holes as shown and insert skewers
Cut out doors and seating space as shown

2. Fix steering wheel and base,
headlights and bumper
with glue

3. Fix hubcap and wheel with glue

15mm

4. Paint the pieces and
click together. Clear
plastic makes a good
windscreen.

Happy driving!

Minton Goes!

TRUCKING

'*B eep beep beep*,' Minton burbled in his sleep.

'If you want a job,' the man at the building site had said, 'you'll need a dump truck.'

Minton longed to shovel and dig. He yearned to scoop and carry. He had already made the truck, but how would the dumper lift up?

'*Heave slide dump*,' he panted through his dreams.

'Sssh!' hissed Turtle in the dark, giving him a prod. But Minton went on beeping and dumping.

In the morning Minton sprang up and clapped Turtle on the shell. 'I've got it!' he cried. 'I know exactly how to do it! I saw it all in a dream.'

'The best thing to do with a dream,' said Turtle, 'is to forget it. Listen to me, I know.'

But Minton was already out the door.

He headed for the caravan park where the beetle trainer lived.

'Have you had breakfast yet?' the trainer asked suspiciously.

'Oh yes, yes, thank you!' said Minton.

He tried not to look too closely at the beetles. They made his mouth water. Beetle *sauce*.

'The thing is, you see,' Minton went on quickly, 'I want to borrow something from your act.'

'Oh?' said the trainer. He was busy teaching a beetle called Rolf to do a full spin on the trapeze. Rolf looked nervous. The trainer gave him a push.

'Catch her by the front legs!' he urged Rolf, as the beetle swung through the air to meet his partner, Babette.

Minton eyed the swing with enthusiasm.

'That's a magnificent trapeze,' he said. 'What's it made of — paperclips?'

'That's right,' said the trainer, trying to untangle the beetles' legs. 'Flippin' feelers!'

'Well, could I have one? A paperclip, that is. I only need one.'

While the beetle trainer went to find a spare, Minton looked at Rolf. Rolf looked at Minton. 'Beetle sauce,' thought Minton.

Minton carried the paperclip carefully back to the caravan. Turtle opened an eye.

'Bingo!' said Minton, holding up his treasure. 'Here's my dumping lever!'

Turtle closed an eye. 'That thing'll never work and you'll get caught beneath it and the dumper will come crashing down and you'll be flattened like a mosquito. But don't listen to me, will you. You never do.'

Minton rummaged through his toolbox and found a fine wooden skewer. He hummed softly as he opened the paperclip and stuck it to the skewer. Then he flipped one end of the clip up and down. It tipped the dumper perfectly. He flipped it again. Easy as snapping your fingers.

'I could do this all afternoon!' crowed Minton.

'You'd better not,' said Turtle, 'or we'll never get the job.'

'Does that mean your coming with me?'

'I suppose so,' said Turtle, yawning. '*Some*one has to earn a living around here.'

At the building site, a new house was going up.
An excavator was demolishing the concrete gutter, to
make a driveway. Minton and Turtle climbed down
from their truck and the foreman called them over.

'See this sand heap?' said the foreman. 'I want you to build castles, big ones, with turrets and a moat and bridges and tunnels. There's a lot of sand to move – think you can do it?'

'Are you joking?' asked Turtle. 'That's easy-peasy for an expert like Minton.'

Just then the long mechanical arm of the excavator swung round and reached out towards Turtle.

'*Aaargh!*' Turtle was scooped up with a load of broken concrete. His shell scraped against the sharp teeth of the bucket. Turtle was lurching higher and higher into the sky. Any minute he was going to be dropped – like a pebble from a cliff.

Suddenly the excavator swivelled round and he was flung to the other side of the bucket. He peered through the spiky teeth. The ground looked very far away. He could hardly see Minton's yellow spots. Then he felt the bucket grinding beneath him. It was starting to split open, ready to empty its load!

'Turtle soup!' he wailed.

Minton scrambled up into the cabin of the excavator. 'Stop!' he cried to the driver. 'Stop! Your machine has swallowed my friend!'

The driver lowered the bucket and turned off the engine. He peered in and poked Turtle's shell with his finger.

'Sorry, mate,' he said, rubbing his chin. 'Thought you were just a rock.'

Turtle sniffed and crawled out. 'Just a rock! He's got rocks in his *head* if you ask me,' he told Minton.

Minton worked all afternoon. Turtle helped him
load up the truck and Minton dumped great piles
of sand to make the skyscraper castles.

They dug lakes and rivers and made islands of
smooth pebbles, joined by bridges. Lights were
beginning to shine in the houses around them, just
as they were finishing.

'Good work,' said the foreman. 'That's just what I need to make people stop and look at my sign.'

BOB BUTTON BUILDS BEST

'*Minton and Turtle Do All the Hard Work*, it should say,' muttered Turtle.

As Minton and Turtle drove back to their caravan, Turtle sighed.

'Are you tired?' asked Minton.

'Yes, even my shell is aching,' said Turtle. 'But don't mind about me, I'm used to being exhausted. No, the worst thing was working with that sand today. It made me homesick. Didn't it make you think of our beach? Don't you miss it?'

Now Minton sighed. 'Yes,' he said quietly. 'I do.'

'Me too. I miss the feel of the sea, all slippery and cool, and napping under the palm trees. What do you miss most?'

'I miss the mornings,' said Minton. 'Raking through the sand. Seeing what has washed up. Lying in my hammock, looking at the stars.'

They both sighed.

'But we can never get back,' Turtle said gloomily. 'We're so far away.'

Minton drove home through the city traffic. He tooted his horn and stopped at the red lights and waved politely at the policeman. But he was frowning. This was the biggest problem he'd ever had.

As they walked back towards the circus, an idea
swam like a bright fish right into his mind.

'Turtle,' he cried. 'I've got it!'

'Uh oh,' said Turtle, but he almost smiled.

This time we won't go over the water. We'll go
under! I'm going to build a submarine to take
us home.'

'It'll never work,' said Turtle. But Minton was already wondering what he could use for a periscope.

How to make Minton's truck

To make Minton's truck you'll need: 2 margarine or butter tubs, a box about the same width, 4 lids, a cork, 2 skewers, 2 icy-pole sticks, a large paperclip, tape, glue, scissors or a sharp knife, and paint.

1. Make holes in tub and insert skewers

2. Unfold paperclip and tape to skewer as shown

3. Cut, fold and tape cabin, and insert front axle

4. Tape icy-pole sticks to cabin and tray

4. Drill holes in lids, paint pieces, and glue cork hubcaps and wheels. Add bumper and assemble

Happy trucking!